First Experiences

By Kira Holmes

First Experiences was first produced by Wolf Pack Theatre
Company on 6th October 2023, Hull

'Life can be rather funny. The good stuff, and the bad. Overall, it's just very therapeutic to find humour within life itself'

Kira Holmes

Characters

KATHERINE, party person of the group

LAURIE, Ex partner to Katherine

ETHAN, the odd one of the group

JESS, identifies as bisexual, socially awkward at times

HOLLY, identifies as asexual, Katherines cousin and overall sarcastic but sensible one

Characters multi roles

KATHERINE; Dimple girl, Jess's mother, Chloe

LAURIE; Holly's sister, Holly's father, Derrick

ETHAN; Tyler, Matt, Adam

JESS; Holly's mother, Dylan

HOLLY; Carrie Lang, Maya, Amy

Notes on the script

The use of props, set moving and multirole is used heavily (whether this be directed in a serious or satirical manner) to tell each character's individual stories.

It is heavily suggested that actors limit their stage exiting and instead integrate background acting when not in multirole

LAURIE
In front of the mirror, getting ready for the party

Don't mind me, just sorting my hair out for tonight. I assume you're coming along too? You know the house we're going to tonight? Yeah, I've had sex in that house. In at least three different rooms. Didn't lose my virginity there though, but we'll get round to that. My first time…
Did I feel different after my first time? Yeah, sweaty! And I guess less innocent. I'm sure everyone feels that way when they do it. But I'll never forget my first, that memory is ingrained into my brain. But this story isn't just about me, I'm sure there's others out there who have experienced the same agony as me. Speaking of agony, I'm stuck going to a party tonight. My ex girlfriends to be exact. I can only hope there's plenty of other people there to hide behind throughout the night.

LAURIE exits the stage to get ready

1

*KATHERINE is on stage, getting ready
for her party*

                 KATHERINE
      Babe… babe!... HOLLY! (HOLLY joins
                   her)

                  HOLLY
      What! I'm here, Christ, stop calling
       me babe, you know it annoys me

                 KATHERINE
              Do I look good?

                  HOLLY
            Yeah,you look fine

                 KATHERINE
                  Fine?

                  HOLLY
                  Yeah…

                 KATHERINE
      I need more than fine Holly!

                  HOLLY
            Fine! You look great!

KATHERINE
No, you've said it now. Clearly I need
to go change my hair or outfit

HOLLY
Eurgh Katherine stop, you don't need
to change

KATHERINE
It's my party Holly, I need to look
good. I reckon a lot of people are
going to show up, it's like the last
party of the summer before everyone
fucks off to university. So stupid…

HOLLY
Stupid?

KATHERINE
Yeah, it's bullshit. Everyone thinking
it's cool or indie to move away to get
into shit loads of debt for some
shitty degree in something they can't
get a job in, like musical theatre or
business

HOLLY
You know I'm doing a musical theatre
degree, if you're going to have a dig
can't you soften the blow a bit?

KATHERINE
But it is a waste of money

HOLLY *is disgruntled, they clearly have already had this conversation before*

KATHERINE
To the audience
I am right, it is a waste of money.
Why would I make the effort to move
and go back into education when I can
be young and enjoy myself, not
worrying about any crappy exams

HOLLY
That reminds me, did you ever hear
back from Manchester?

KATHERINE doesn't respond

HOLLY
Did you get another rejection?

KATHERINE
I didn't want to go there anyways. I
only applied there because you're
going there. My mum made me, I think
she thought it would be a good idea
going to the same place as you. But
just because you're my cousin doesn't
mean I'd be hanging out with you there

                    HOLLY
                (sarcastically)
         Yeah, because we never hang out
         together usually. Not sure what its
         called what we're doing right now

                    KATHERINE
              You know what I mean

                    HOLLY
         Well you need to get your act together
         and figure out what you're going to do

                    KATHERINE
         Nope, not having this conversation
         with you. Come on, help me get the
         drinks out. People should be arriving
                    soon

         *Set change to the living room, HOLLY
         is welcoming JESS. KATHERINE joins*

                    JESS
                    Hey!

                    KATHERINE
              Where are Amy and Chloe?

                    JESS
         At uni? They left a few days ago?

KATHERINE
Eurgh, they're the fun ones…

to the audience

I mean don't get me wrong, Jess is
fun. I just don't know her as much as
the others. She's nice, she's just not
very exciting, or adventurous. From
what I heard of anyway…

To JESS

Let me go get you a drink

(KATHERINE exits)

JESS
What's her problem?

HOLLY
She got rejected from Manchester

JESS
Amy said that she didn't want to go to
university

HOLLY
So she says. I heard you got into
Leeds, when do you go?

                    JESS
       Next Monday, I'm so excited. So who
           else is coming to the party?

                    HOLLY
         You know what, I actually don't know

KATHERINE enters

                  KATHERINE
       Ok! So here's your drink, and here is
        your welcome shot! I have like 50
         lined up in the kitchen ready for
                    everyone

(KATHERINE passes the shot to JESS,
who proceeds to take it)

                    JESS
        So is anyone else coming that I know?

                  KATHERINE
        Well I just pressed the button on
       facebook that said invite all, so who
       knows? But my aim is to get Holly laid
             before she goes away

(HOLLY looks uncomfortable at this
thought, we hear a knock on the door)

KATHERINE
Just walk in!

LAURIE enters sheepishly

KATHERINE
Oh, Hi

LAURIE
Hi

HOLLY & JESS:
Awkwardly
Hi…

LAURIE
So are other people out back?

HOLLY
We're the only ones here

KATHERINE
For now, I'm sure plenty of other
people will show up. Anyways, why did
you even come?

LAURIE
Why did you invite me?

Pause

                    JESS
    Are you going to get him his welcome
                    shot?

                  KATHERINE
    Not now Jess! I need to go sort out
              the kitchen

KATHERINE leaves

                   HOLLY
    That's not awkward at all. How have
             you been Laurie?

                   LAURIE
    Good, yeah. Just been busy packing
    for the move. Maybe I shouldn't be
    here. These parties are usually really
    busy, I was kind of hoping to hide in
          a corner. I should go

                   HOLLY
    No don't go, once we've got a few
    drinks down us, I'm sure Katherine
    will start to relax. I think the break
          up is still a bit raw

                    JESS
    Didn't you both break up like two
               months ago?

                    HOLLY
         How about I get us all some more
                  drinks, yeah?

*HOLLY goes to get more drinks as JESS
and LAURIE stand awkwardly making
small talk.*

KATHERINE comes back with HOLLY

                  KATHERINE
         (Whispers) Why is he here?

                    HOLLY
         I think at the current moment you
         can't complain about the people who
         have turned up to your party, you
                know… all two of them

                  KATHERINE
         I don't want to talk to him

                    HOLLY
         Look, I'm going to say this in the
         most loving way. You're not together
         anymore, put on your big girl knickers
         on and go talk to your guests. I'm not
                  the party host

                  KATHERINE
                    Fine!

KATHERINE walks to LAURIE and passes him his drink

                    KATHERINE:
              There you go

                     LAURIE
                     Beer?

                    KATHERINE
                      Yes

                     LAURIE
                  Budweiser?

                    KATHERINE
                     Yepp

                     LAURIE:
        Thanks, that's my favourite beer

                    KATHERINE
                    I know

                      JESS
          So are people excited for uni?

                    KATHERINE
          Nope, no university talk. Only fun
                     stuff

                     LAURIE
                     Like?

KATHERINE
I don't know, a game?

JESS
Never have I ever?

KATHERINE
Good idea! Never have I ever…

There is a knock on the door

KATHERINE
Come in!

ETHAN enters
ETHAN
Yes then! Party time!

KATHERINE
Oh, Nathan?

ETHAN
Ethan actually. Hi everyone!

(He takes KATHERINE's drink out of her hand, takes a sip)

ETHAN
White wine spritzer? What are you, a 40 year old stay at home mum?

KATHERINE
Hey!

ETHAN
Can you go get me some real alcohol

KATHERINE
Erm, sure. Holly come with?

HOLLY follows her of stage

HOLLY
You invited weird Ethan?

KATHERINE
I told you, I pressed invite all. I
didn't even know I had him on
facebook!

LAURIE
Hey man, how are you doing?

ETHAN
Yeah good, thought there'd be more
people here tonight. Anyone know if
Carrie Lang is coming?

JESS
Carrie Lang, thought she'd be too cool
to stick around here to hang out with
people like us

                    ETHAN
             So is this everyone?

                    LAURIE
        I think so, looks like it's going to
        be a quiet one. Glad I'm not the only
        guy here now. Thanks for coming man.

                    ETHAN
        Yeah don't worry, we'll have a great
        night. Get pissed and get laid, that's
        usually the deal with these parties

                    LAURIE
        Ok, calm down now. It's just a regular
                    party

                    ETHAN
        So what's your deal Jess? You're
                    single?

                    JESS
                    Yeah…

                    ETHAN
        Are you straight? Looking for any fun
                    tonight?

*KATHERINE and HOLLY come back with
drinks*

KATHERINE
Ok, let's play the game while we wait
for others to arrive

LAURIE:
But Katherine, The start time for the
party was an hour ago

*HOLLY elbows him in hope that he will
stop talking*

JESS
Ok, never have I ever. I'll start.
Never have I ever stolen something…

Some drink

HOLLY
Never have I ever started a fight

*KATHERINE drinks, LAURIE rolls his
eyes*

LAURIE
Never have I ever been with more than
one person during sex

ETHAN drinks, everybody looks at him

KATHERINE
Erm, wait. Did you hear the question
right?

ETHAN
Yeah

KATHERINE
...ok

ETHAN
Never have I ever made out with three
different girls on a night out
(*ETHAN drinks*)

KATHERINE
Ethan, do you know how to play this
game?

ETHAN
Yeah

KATHERINE
When it's your turn you're meant to
say something you've never done and
not drink, you know because you
haven't done it

ETHAN
But what if you have done it?

KATHERINE
But you haven't

ETHAN
But how do you know I haven't?

KATHERINE
I just know Ethan…

ETHAN
Fine. Don't believe me

JESS
Ok, never have I ever regretted
sleeping with someone

HOLLY takes a sip of her drink

KATHERINE
But you've only had sex with one
person. Was he bad?

HOLLY
No, no he was a nice guy

ETHAN
But she's not denying it was bad

HOLLY
It's not as simple as that. I'm just,
not into sex

KATHERINE
Not into sex? Is that a real thing?
Everyone is into sex, it's human
nature. That's what sexuality is…

HOLLY
Sexuality, it's a funny thing, I've
never fully understood it, for a long
time I thought there was something
wrong with me.
It's not easy. I can't just say to you
all that my first time was rose petals
and tingly lube. It just wasn't for
me. I think I'm on a journey, I'm
trying to discover myself but the more
I search the more lost I get. The more
I try the more I'm unsure, how does
that work? You know when you're a
teenager and you start getting the
urges and you think oh well if I stick
my finger there it feels good and that
crap? Yeah (pause) I never got that.
My younger sister would run into my
room with her latest poster from a
magazine and say…

HOLLY'S SISTER
Oh, Holly don't you think Justin
Bieber is beautiful!

HOLLY
Or even…

HOLLY'S SISTER
Hmm I like older men now; like I could
adopt 50 kids too for Brad Pitts dick

HOLLY
Even now she still finds a sexual
attraction to some weird famous men

HOLLY'S SISTER
I LOVE John Barrowman!

HOLLY
You know he's married... to a man?

HOLLY'S SISTER
I don't care! Once he meets me, he'll
realise he's not gay and we'll have
two children and he'll sing to them
every night. You know he can sing? I
got like three of his CD's already.
And Oh my God did you see him in
Doctor Who? YUM! I heard he's going to
be on I'm a celeb, I'm totally voting
for him

HOLLY
She would get so over excited and
spent way too much time in her room
during this phase. I just didn't get
it, and I don't think she did either.
She'd always question me about who I
fancied, which celeb I want to do. One
of her favourites was snog, marry,
kill. It got even more difficult when
she was about fifteen…

HOLLY'S SISTER
Holly, what does it feel like to touch
a penis?

HOLLY
Erm…..

HOLLY'S SISTER
Because Aaron wants me to touch it and
like I'm just not sure what to expect.
I know the tip looks like a mushroom
and I went on the embarrassing bodies
website but I'm still a bit unsure

HOLLY
You know you don't have to touch it if
you don't want too

HOLLY's SISTER
Oh course I want to touch it, I'm just
asking what it's like

HOLLY
I don't know what it's like, ok?

HOLLY'S SISTER
Oh… Well that's a bit weird isn't it?

HOLLY
That's right, I was seventeen and I
had never touched a penis or vagina
and I didn't want to either. Was that
weird? Was I weird? Isn't it weird to
want to touch it? I mean have you seen
genitals? Not very inviting…

I mean have you seen a penis, it looks
like a parsnip

JESS
More like a mushroom

LAURIE
Maybe a carrot

ETHAN
Cucumber

KATHERINE
Vaginas aren't any better, it looks
like a peach

JESS
An apple

HOLLY
Yeah, like an onion… because of the
layers

Cast stare at her

There was no attraction to it. But all
my friends were crazy about it all,
dick pics were flying everywhere. They
kept telling me that something will
kick start my sexual drive. Maybe they
were right, I just needed to find
something that worked for me.
Let me tell you, the categories on
Pornhub are plentiful. I was almost
proud of society for being so diverse
with their porn. So, I'm scrolling
through videos; amateur, fetish,
lesbian, gangbangs, even MILFs… and
nothing. I felt nothing! What was
wrong with my vagina, what did it
want? Why was I not like everyone
else? I grew tired of the comments and
questions people threw at me. I
remember one friend saying…

TYLER
Don't knock it till you've tried it

HOLLY
But I didn't want to try it! I mean, I
wouldn't object to having someone in
my life. But it seemed like to have
that aspect you'd have to be willing
to put out. My friends believed it was
an important part of any relationship,
but why did it have too?

I gave into societies social
conventions and rules. I thought… Fuck
it! I'm going to go get me some dick
and see if I like it. And if I don't
then I'm a lesbian, because apparently
there are only two options.
I wasn't bothered either way, I just
wanted to understand myself. So, I
text my friend Tyler and I'm all like…
'Hey, can I come over? I'll order
pizza' and he's all like….

TYLER
Yeah sure, but X-Factors on so we
gotta watch that first

HOLLY
Tyler was a nice guy, he'd been my
friend for a few years now. I knew I
could trust him, I mean I wasn't
sexually attracted to him but if I had
to do it then he was probably the best
choice at that time

                    HOLLY
       So, there I am, just us two in the
    house. We sat on his sofa watching the
       shitty X-Factor auditions. And I
     thought yeah let's just get this over
      with. I mean, I didn't know how to
     start it so I just placed my hand on
               his crotch gently

                    TYLER
             Erm… you ok there?

                    HOLLY
                 Yeah fine

                    TYLER
         You know your hands on my dick?

                    HOLLY
                  Yepp…

                    TYLER
           Ok, as long as you know that

                    HOLLY
                   Sex…

                    TYLER
                   What?

                    HOLLY
      Let's have sex? Good old fashioned
            penis in vagina fun?

                    TYLER
                 Erm, what?

                    HOLLY
    I want sex now Tyler. Please? (Almost
          questioning her please)

                    TYLER
    Ok, but can I put X-Factor on pause?

                    HOLLY
              Erm yeah, sure

                    TYLER
    Just the auditions are the best part

                    HOLLY
       Tyler just take your pants off

                    TYLER
                   Ok...

HOLLY

So, he was on top of me, sweating like
he's running a marathon, the poor guy.
And pulling these faces, like maybe he
might sneeze on me? I'm not sure. But
I'm just laying on the sofa wondering
if any of the judges on X-Factor are
going to press that golden buzzer or
not. A few more minutes passed,
cheekily checking the time on my
watch. Jeez the guy was taking
forever. I mean how long was sex meant
to last. It got a bit quicker, and he
started saying my name…

TYLER
Hmmm Holly, Yes…say my name…

HOLLY
Yes… Tyler. You're…doing good?

HOLLY

And with that he finished, the entire
situation felt wrong to me. I knew
deep down I didn't want to do this. It
wasn't for me. He got up and pulled
his pants back on, unpaused X-Factor
and grabbed the last slice of the
pepperoni pizza. So, hey, I tried, and
it just wasn't my cup of tea. I'm sure
any other girl Tyler would have made a
good impression, but me. So, I sat
down and said 'Tyler, I think
something's wrong with me, I don't
like sex'

TYLER

Oh cool, ok. Did you know that before
or was it me?

HOLLY

It wasn't you Tyler. I'm sorry but I
just needed to see, and I wanted it to
be with a person I trusted. He looked
hurt

(Tyler reacts)

HOLLY

I then realised at that moment that I broke that trust. I used him, and because of that I hated myself that tiny bit more. I left his house, I didn't really know what else to do. All I remember is that it created a million more questions for me. Why did I feel I had to do this?

Fast forward to the lovely age of eighteen. Still sexually confused, just one year older. I started sixth form studying sociology. And there was this girl across the room, short brown bob, large blue eyes and an infectious grin that showed her dimples off nicely. I saw her a few weeks after on a night out around town and got talking to her. I asked, "Are there any good-looking guys out there for you tonight?" I mean that's what girls are meant to talk about right? This was the social norm of talking to a fellow female. And she was like…

DIMPLE GIRL

Nah, they aren't my type

HOLLY

Well who was?

                    DIMPLE GIRL
              girls, preferably short one

                       HOLLY
           To which I thought… cool. This girl
         knows what she wants, good for her. At
         least someone had confidence in some
            aspect of their life. She wasn't
         chasing after a partner like my other
          friends, so I just chilled out with
            her for the night. It was a good
          night, by the time it hit 3am most of
          my friends had gone home or found
          someone to go home with. Leaving me
                  with her. She said…

                    DIMPLE GIRL
         Let's share a taxi, we can go back to
         mine and have another drink, it's
                  still early yet

                       HOLLY
           I mean sweetie, it's 3am in the
         morning, but okay. We ended up having
          this insightful talk about life and
           the journey she went on when she
             explored her own sexuality.

                    DIMPLE GIRL
                So what's your deal?

                    HOLLY
            I don't have a deal

                 DIMPLE GIRL
            Everyone has a deal

                    HOLLY
              Nope, not me

        (The female character approaches her)

                    HOLLY
    I remember she kept getting closer and
      closer to me, it started to feel
                uncomfortable

                 DIMPLE GIRL
    So, you wouldn't be into me kissing
                    you?

                    HOLLY
            Erm, not really…

                 DIMPLE GIRL
    So, it wouldn't turn you on having a
    guy or girl with their head between
                your legs?

HOLLY
If anything, seeing someone's head
between my legs makes me think about
how weird it is that babies' heads are
there too when they're born. Look I'm
sorry but it wasn't doing anything for
me

DIMPLE GIRL
Oh ok, how about this?

(Character jokingly reveals a
prosthetic penis)

HOLLY
Oh ok. Look I'm sorry but this is just
getting uncomfortable

DIMPLE GIRL
I'm sorry, I'm only having a mess
around, jeez everyone has one. So,
what are you? Straight, gay,
bi-sexual?

HOLLY
I'm not any of them. Why is this so
difficult to understand!? It's like a
barrier stopping me from normality. I
just needed to face the fact that I
didn't feel sexual attraction.

HOLLY
I'm sure I could have had a happy
emotional relationship with Tyler or
had a lot of fun with dimple girl. But
I just couldn't, I needed someone like
me. Someone I can share my life with,
without the expectation of sex. Surely
there were people out there that were
like me. It got to a point when my
parents started questioning me,
wondering when I'm going to bring
anyone home. I said to them, look I've
had a long hard think and typed some
stuff into google, and I believe I'm
asexual. Finding an answer was a
weight off my shoulders, it felt like
it changed my life. My dad was
thrilled…

HOLLY'S DAD
Yes! That's one less daughter that
might get accidentally knocked up by
some idiot

HOLLY
He says having two daughters that were
both unplanned?
I remember my mum was confused…

HOLLY'S MUM
Are you sure you're not just a
feminist?

HOLLY
I'm now aware of how oppressive some
traditional concepts of womanhood are.
My sexual orientation is irrelevant,
I'm a good person and just because I'm
asexual doesn't mean I'm not normal.
People need to understand that it
isn't a choice, it's not a problem to
be fixed. I'm not sorry I don't have a
typical story of shagging someone at
camp or losing it to my childhood
sweetheart. But if you're wondering
how I lost my virginity then there you
go. My bad Tyler, I've figured it out
now

As people say…We are in the era of
snowflakes, and fuck me am I going to
take advantage of being in a time
where I can be myself.

KATHERINE
Wow, I didn't know that was a thing.
Why didn't you tell me?

HOLLY
I didn't think it was a big deal.
It's cool if people want to talk about
that part of their life so openly. I'm
just not part of those people, and
that's ok too.

                    JESS
   But if you think about it, if you
   never slept with Tyler then you
   wouldn't know you was asexual

                   HOLLY
   I think I always knew, I just needed
   to discover it myself. I don't regret
   sleeping with Tyler because it was
   bad. I regret it because it was a
   shitty thing for me to do, using him
                 like that.

                    ETHAN
   He's a bloke, I don't think he regrets
                    it

                  KATHERINE
   Shut up Ethan, you don't know what
   you're on about. You've probably never
   even been close to getting a girl

                    ETHAN
   I'll let you know I've had sex
                  actually

                  KATHERINE
             Ok with who?

                    ETHAN
              Carrie Lang

KATHERINE
Bull shit

LAURIE
Alright Katherine, you can be a bit
nicer

KATHERINE
Nicer? You just like to disagree with
everything I say. You constantly did
it when we were together. But it's
true, he's talking utter bull shit.

ETHAN
It's not bullshit, is it Laurie?

LAURIE
I mean not from what you've told me

KATHERINE
You're just sticking up for your mate.
There's no way you've slept with
anyone Ethan, you're so full of shit

ETHAN
Well it was at one of your parties

KATHERINE
In my house!?

ETHAN
Yepp, in a bed

KATHERINE
Which bed?

ETHAN
I don't think I need to say

KATHERINE
Which bed Ethan!?

ETHAN
Let's just say one of the things me
and Laurie have in common is what bed
we've had sex on (*ETHAN goes to high
five LAURIE*)

LAURIE
Nope, you're on your own there mate

KATHERINE
Wait, you knew about this? On my bed!

LAURIE
Look, you've had a lot of parties. I'm
sure plenty of people have boned on
your bed. Also I don't even know if
it's true.

ETHAN
It is true! Me and Carrie have been
playing cat and mouse with each other
all through school. She was my first,
we loved each other. Well, so I
thought

ETHAN

Carrie Lang, the beauty to my beast…
the princess Peach to my Mario. Rachel
to my Ross. I first laid my eyes on
this stunning creature in year seven,
it was during P.E. They used to
separate the boys and girls in the gym
hall with this big ass net, so we
didn't get 'distracted'. So we're
playing dodgeball and LAURIE whams
this ball straight at me, I whack it
away and it rolls into the girls side
of the hall. I ran over and it was
basically like slow motion, she smiled
at me, revealing her adorable purple
braces, her ponytail swished as she
turned around. She was an angel in gym
shorts. I even remember the first
thing she ever said to me

CARRIE LANG

Fuck off Perv before I get Miss Rayman

ETHAN

Definitely banter, her head was
telling me to leave but I bet her
heart was saying something else. Her
eyes begged me to stay. But I played
it cool and waved goodbye to her. She
responded with her middle finger…

                    ETHAN
     In year eight I sat behind her in
   history class, and she awoke all my
  senses with her heavenly presence. The
  back of her head was so beautiful, I'd
     stare at it for the entire class.
   Sometimes she would lean back on her
  chair and I was lucky enough to get a
    whiff of her hair, the smell of
  coconut got me through my day. We got
  put into groups to discuss the battle
  of Hastings and thankfully we were put
    together….it felt like destiny. She
      pulled her chair next to me and
   slumped back. As our group talked and
  answered the questions on the sheet, I
  watched her in all her natural beauty.
   She just sat there… picking a loose
  hair out of her gum. That year she had
    green braces, it was a bold choice.
  But she suited any colour. She didn't
  want to do any work but that's fine,
  royalty don't have to work, they have
  more important things to worry about.
  If my princess didn't want to do any
  work that's fine. She pushed the sheet
            across to me and said

                 CARRIE LANG
  You're a nerd, you can answer that
                   shit

ETHAN

She thought I was smart! And to know I
was smart she must have been watching
me answer the questions in class or
listening to what I was saying. What
if she was asking people about me and
they said I was smart. Why was she
asking people about me? Was she
interested?

CARRIE LANG

Hurry up Nathan before time runs out

ETHAN

It's Ethan actually. I can't believe
she almost got my name right; my
adrenaline was at an all time high!
She must honestly be interested in me.
This cat and mouse game continued…
Year nine came around and I'm in the
social area with Laurie just chilling
and eating my pack up, and through the
window I can see her in netball
practice in her cute skirt. She runs,
spins and jumps.

LAURIE

God Grant us our prayers and let a
gust of wind blow up her skirt and
reveal some kinky underwear...

ETHAN
You do know they wear shorts
underneath…

LAURIE
They wear fucking shorts underneath,
what a con!

ETHAN
Laurie wasn't happy, but I did get to
see her on the netball court smiling
while showing off her new blue braces
and that's enough to make any boy over
excited. I sat on the bench with my
muller corner yogurt and my jaw
hanging. I didn't realise I drooled
the yogurt all over my jumper until
Laurie pointed it out

LAURIE
Oy mate, it looks like you've been
cummed on by the fucking rugby team
the amount you've spilled on yourself

ETHAN
Then my worst nightmare happened. She
started dating a guy in the year
above. Dylan, what kind of name is
Dylan? Dylan the fucking dildo…

ETHAN

Anyways, she's dating this twat and all he does is kiss her and grab her butt like she's a piece of meat. Worst of all she looks like she's enjoying it. Unless… she was pretending to enjoy it to get my attention, that may be a possibility. He was just a full on prick, his facebook profile picture was him topless posing with his dog. How am I meant to compete with that!? A hot muscly guy with a stupidly cute dog? It was mission impossible mate I tell you. I mean I tried to do the same thing and changed my profile picture to me and my lizard, but it didn't get me anywhere. I remember walking down the corridor one day and they're snogging against a wall, I notice he runs his hands up her top and starts playing with her chest. I didn't mean to stare, and let me tell you… he wasn't happy when he noticed

CARRIE LANG

What the fuck you looking at dickhead?

ETHAN

Nothing…

LAURIE

You know you make it obvious when you stare at them

ETHAN
I can't help it

LAURIE
Ethan you look like you either want to
be him or be in him, which is it

ETHAN
Neither!

LAURIE
Oh please, you'd give your left
testicle to be him

ETHAN
Laurie was right. I got home later
that day and laid in bed feeling sorry
for myself. I closed my eyes and
imagined it was me doing that, kissing
her and running my fingers through her
hair

LAURIE
Best wank of your fucking life

ETHAN
Excuse me… but yes it was

(ETHAN alludes to this thought before
moving onto the next part)

ETHAN

But then year eleven came round, and
that was my year. I mean I spent most
of it watching them both together. But
just before the school year was up, he
cheated on her with big boobs Bella in
his year and it broke her heart. She
boasted about bringing him to prom,
but she just ended up going with her
friends, she looked miserable the
whole night. I wanted to go over, but
I just didn't have the courage. I
decided to wait until the after-prom
party that Katherine was having. She
basically invited the entire year, but
I knew that was my chance to tell her
that I loved her.

I remember that night so well, you
could hear the music all the way down
the street. I walked through the door
and the first thing I was greeted with
was Katherine running into the front
garden to vomit

KATHERINE
Vomit sound

ETHAN
And Laurie followed her out to make
sure she was ok, he was pretty pissed
off she got herself in a state so
early in the night.

KATHERINE
Laurie babe, can you look after me
sweetie

ETHAN
I grabbed a beer from the kitchen and
wandered around the crowded house to
look for Carrie, after looking
downstairs I was worried she didn't
turn up to the party. Until I heard
her sobbing at the top of the stairs.

LAURIE
She basically walked in on Dylan
balls deep in her best mate

ETHAN
Will you please stop! Anyways, I
didn't really know what to say to her,
I just kneeled next to her and asked
if she was ok.

CARRIE LANG
DO I FUCKING LOOK OK?

ETHAN
I helped her up, lead her to the
kitchen and poured her a few shots

CARRIE LANG
Men are the fucking worse you know,
like what's their problem? Why can't
you guys be happy with one girl?

ETHAN
I don't know

CARRIE LANG
You have a cock, you must know

ETHAN
We're not all the same

CARRIE LANG
You are, I swear I should just be a
lesbian. At least my heart wouldn't
get broken

ETHAN
I mean it could still happen… Women
can also break your heart. But Carrie,
you gotta realise how wonderful you
are. Dylan's a dick, you deserve the
world

CARRIE LANG
Really?

                    ETHAN
Carrie if we were stood outside, you'd
out shine all the stars in the night
                     sky

   And with that she kissed me, she
   finally kissed me! That night was
   magical, and I'll never forget it.
   That's the night I lost my virginity,
   the first time (dramatic pause) I made
   love to a girl. She left quite quickly
   after it though, I assumed she wanted
   to leave the party on a good note. I
   went to visit her the next day, I
   knocked on her front door and as it
   opened her beautiful face appeared…

                  CARRIE LANG
   What the fuck are you doing here?

                    ETHAN
   I thought we could do something today,
   share an ice cream or even go bowling?

                  CARRIE LANG
   How the hell do you know where I live?

                    ETHAN
                    Erm…

                  CARRIE LANG
   Nathan that's so creepy

ETHAN
It's Ethan

CARRIE LANG
Just leave me alone

ETHAN
And with that she shut the door. I
knew what game she was playing, she
wanted me to prove my love for her.
Like a knight wooing a princess, I
could do that. I researched all night,
watched a lot of rom coms and read a
few of my mum's magazines. I knew what
to do, I had the perfect plan. Has
anyone seen that movie 'Say Anything'?

LAURIE
John Laurie is a fucking legend

ETHAN
He holds a boombox up to her bedroom
window, and it works like a charm. But
I mean, we're in the 21st Century.
Where the hell would I find a boombox
from? I made do with what I had, my
phone…and a Bluetooth speaker. I held
it up to her window

CARRIE LANG
Nathan, what the hell are you doing?

ETHAN
It's Ethan… and Carrie Lang I love
you!

CARRIE LANG
What!?

ETHAN
I love you with all my heart, I have
loved you since Year 7, and when we're
old sitting in our armchairs next to
the fireplace watching over our
Grandchildren, I'll still love you
then!

CARRIE LANG
I swear I'll call the police

ETHAN
You don't have to pretend anymore
Carrie, I know you love me! We can be
together, forever. Just say you love
me!

CARRIE LANG
I don't love you!

ETHAN
Yes you do!

CARRIE LANG
No I FUCKING DON'T!

ETHAN
She didn't love me… she broke my
heart. I had the police visit me the
same day telling me to leave her alone
or she'd take a restraining order out
on me.
I'll never forget you Carrie Lang…

You've taught me so much, I know now
that I can't obsess over a person who
isn't interested in me, it's not
healthy. I shouldn't have obsessed
over you when you blatantly showed no
interest in me, I bet you still don't
remember my name. I'll admit, I've
learnt my lesson. But I know now that
I should wait for someone who likes
me, that's what I deserve in life. I'm
just going to enjoy my youth, my mum
said that any girl would be lucky to
have me. Was kinda hoping for more
girls here tonight if I'm honest. You
know, for emotional healing purposes.

JESS
You're still emotionally healing after
two years?

KATHERINE
Bull Shit!

                         ETHAN
         Why don't you believe me? I thought
         out of everyone you'd know the pain I
                  felt after being dumped

                       KATHERINE
          I'd know? What do you mean by that

                         ETHAN
            You know, when Laurie dumped you

                       KATHERINE
             Excuse me! That was mutual

                         ETHAN
         Was it? Then why did you spend all day
          crying in between classes that day?

                       KATHERINE
         I wasn't crying! Just shut up Ethan,
          you don't know what you're talking
                        about

                         ETHAN
            Ok, ok stop being hysterical

                        LAURIE
         Alright, alright let's just stop now.
         Don't call her hysterical, let's all
           just sit back down and chill out

                       KATHERINE
                       Thank you

LAURIE gives her a reassuring smile and squeezes her arm to comfort her

ETHAN
Come on you two, get a room

HOLLY
You really don't know how to socialise appropriately do you?

JESS
What is the reason why you both broke up?

HOLLY
Apparently no one knows how to socialise appropriately

LAURIE
We decided that because of university, we wanted to be able to enjoy our experience

KATHERINE
You. You decided that

There is an awkward silence

HOLLY
Hey, why don't we all go for a cigarette or something outside?

JESS
I have a vape, come on let's go

ETHAN
Once I managed to smoke an entire vape
in an hour

JESS
I don't think you did mate…

*They exit, leaving KATHERINE and
LAURIE*

LAURIE
Katherine, you know we've had this
conversation

KATHERINE
What if I want to have it again?

LAURIE
We've been drinking, it's going to end
in a fight

KATHERINE
Maybe I want to fight, maybe I want
to do anything if it means I get one
more moment with you alone before you
go and move away. Even if it means
fighting

LAURIE

You know how difficult it's been these
past few months. But you have to
realise, we were never good together.
We fought, all the time. I was never
enough for you, nothing was. I'm not
sure what you wanted from me, a
partner to be by your side for the
rest of your life?

I can't do that, not at our age. I
want time to grow into the person I'm
meant to be. I need it. I'm not your
dream guy, and do you know why?
Because we're 18, you don't know who
your dream guy is.

You know, a small part of me wants to
be that guy, to stay in this shitty
town. But it's not the right choice
for me to make.

KATHERINE

You know you could stay here, with me.
We can keep trying.

*She gets closer to LAURIE, and goes
in to kiss him*

LAURIE

You don't think I've thought about
that? I have, so many times. But you
deserve new experiences

KATHERINE
I don't care about sleeping with other
people. Are you just wanting to fuck
other girls?

LAURIE
I don't just mean that and anyway you
know I don't think about gender when
it comes to that, and sex isn't
exactly my priority right now. You
don't want to be stuck with me for the
rest of your life. We both need to
have the opportunity to enjoy our
lives, you need to stop being so self
destructive.

KATHERINE
Why don't you just stay the night?
Just one night

LAURIE
You want me to stay the night?

KATHERINE
Do you want to stay the night?

Silence

KATHERINE
You usually go quiet when I'm right

                    LAURIE
It doesn't matter what I want, it's
what's right. We're messy Katherine,
   we have been since we first got
together. We can't get back together

                  KATHERINE
Who says anything about getting back
   together? It's just one night, it
   doesn't mean we're bound for life

                    LAURIE
                 Doesn't it?

We're not kids anymore. We've had
great experiences together. You'll
           always be my first

                  KATHERINE
               First shag?

                    LAURIE
                First love

Pause

                    LAURIE
      Please stop limiting yourself
                 Katherine

KATHERINE
I'll try, and you'll never know. You
might meet the love of your life at
university

LAURIE
Or you'll actually start to enjoy
yourself and find a good looking guy,
who is a decent shag. Obviously won't
be a god in bed like me

KATHERINE
Oh is that what you think our sex life
was like?

LAURIE
Absolutely

Lights down

Interval

HOLLY
Everyone ok?

KATHERINE
Yeah, we're just talking about how
crap..

LAURIE
God like

KATHERINE
Laurie was in bed

JESS
Speaking of bed, we've thought of some
more questions. Come on

They proceed to sit

JESS
Ready? Never have I ever role played
with someone

*KATHERINE and LAURIE look at
eachother and take a sip of their
drink*

JESS
Wait, you both took a drink. So it is
true, was it while you were dating?

LAURIE
You know we don't have to go into it

HOLLY
But I love this story

LAURIE
Do you know about this story?

HOLLY
Obviously, where else do you think she
would have thought that 'never have I
ever'

ETHAN
Are you guys into role play?

KATHERINE
What? No!

LAURIE
It wasn't like a recurring thing, it
only happened once or twice. One being
when we had our first time together

KATHERINE
That time wasn't role play, it was a
costume party!

*They all stare at LAURIE in hope he
will tell the story. He sighs and
gestures to KATHERINE to start*

KATHERINE
Our first time was, what's the word
for not good but not bad

LAURIE
Yeah it was alright

KATHERINE
It was October the 29th

LAURIE
I think it was Halloween maybe, it
would explain the costumes

KATHERINE
It was Mel's costume party. She always
threw the best parties, her mum worked
nights, so we had till 6am to get
pissed, get laid and get out. There
were only like three of us who were
old enough to buy alcohol. So, we all
bummed £20 in for her.

LAURIE
We were swimming in it

KATHERINE
I was so excited when that Facebook
invite came through, so many people
were up for it

LAURIE

I really wasn't up for it, I'm not
much of a party guy But Katherine
convinced me to go. She said it
wouldn't be the same without me there.
But the same thing happened at every
party. We'd walk in, she'd go straight
to her loud friends and start chugging
shots while I stood in the corner of
the kitchen looking after her handbag.
She only spoke to me at a party when
she'd drank too much and wanted to be
taken care of

KATHERINE

He used to take real good care of me
when we went to parties

LAURIE

Anyways so she dragged me to this
stupid costume party

KATHERINE

He was so up for this party

LAURIE

I fucking hate dressing up

KATHERINE

I love dressing up. It took me weeks
to plan my outfit

                    LAURIE
          Best thing I had was a suit

                  KATHERINE
        I needed to look sexy for him

                    LAURIE
      I needed something that let me wear my
                     suit

                  KATHERINE
       I spent a lot of money to look good
                   that night

                    LAURIE
        I wasn't willing to spend money on
             some shitty costume

                  KATHERINE
      I had a feeling that night was going
     to be special, I thought he was the
     one. He'd been so patient with me

                    LAURIE
        My balls had been blue for a few
     months waiting for her to be ready

                  KATHERINE
          I just needed confidence

                    LAURIE
            I just needed alcohol

KATHERINE
I slipped into my costume, a Princess
Jasmin outfit that showed a lot of
skin. Looking back I don't know how
appropriate it was for me to dress as
that character, but my bum looked
great. I would have been slutty red
riding hood but that bitch Rachel
already taxed that idea

LAURIE
I went as the detective from 'Who
Framed Rodger Rabbit'

KATHERINE
He looked good

LAURIE
I looked good

KATHERINE
I met him there, he had a drink
waiting for me

LAURIE
I welcomed her with a beer like a
gentleman

KATHERINE
How could he not remember I fucking
hated beer. Out of all the alcohol
there, he stands at the door with a
bloody beer

LAURIE
I think we'd been together for about 2
months

KATHERINE
we'd been together for 4 months and
10 days

LAURIE
She spoke a lot of crap like what she
wanted in life and serious boring
stuff like that, but she had a good
pair of tits which made up for it

KATHERINE
He was such a good listener… sometimes

LAURIE
a couple of hours into the party, I
got tired of waiting

KATHERINE
An hour and a half into the party he
made his move during a game of twister

LAURIE
I lead her up the stairs like a gent I
am

KATHERINE
He practically yanked me up the
stairs, I knew the costume would work

                    LAURIE
        I was going to blow her mind

                  KATHERINE
    He told me he was going to rock my
                    world

                    LAURIE
    We found an empty room, it was pretty
                    dark

                  KATHERINE
    We sneaked into this weird shaped
    room, like a loft conversion. The
    walls were slopped. Not much space

                    LAURIE
    I closed the door quietly, preparing
          her to scream my name

                  KATHERINE
    He slammed the door shut, bit creepy
        when I think back to it

                    LAURIE
    I kissed her on her lips and neck

KATHERINE
Then all of a sudden, he started
attacking me with his vacuum mouth,
like everywhere (give impression). It
felt like he was trying to suck up the
crumbs from the wotsits I ate 1o
minutes ago and sounded like Nu Nu
from Teletubbies

LAURIE
I even cheekily licked her neck up and
down, you know like what you see in
porn

KATHERINE
He started licking me, and not in the
right places

LAURIE
Up and down

KATHERINE
My vaginas not there you fucking idiot

LAURIE
Bit of side to side

KATHERINE
Why can't you be doing this to my Fu
Fu?

LAURIE
I even added a bit of flickering

KATHERINE
Do this to my fucking pussy!

LAURIE
She fucking loved it so much, she
climbed on top of me

KATHERINE
I needed him to stop, so I climbed on
top of him

LAURIE
She defo wanted to give me a blowy

KATHERINE
I just wanted him to kiss me

LAURIE
I wanted her to know that I didn't
mind her doing it

KATHERINE
He just kept pushing my head down

LAURIE
I just wanted her to stop teasing me

KATHERINE
I gave in, he clearly wanted me to
suck his dick

LAURIE
I mean I washed it and everything for
her

KATHERINE
But I knew I was good at giving
blowjobs

LAURIE
I heard she fucking loved a bit of
cock in her gob

KATHERINE
Just because you're good at something
doesn't mean you enjoy it though

LAURIE
Yeah you could tell from her moans she
fucking loved it

KATHERINE
Added a moan or two while doing it,
makes a man feel good doesn't it?

LAURIE
She was like 'ooh yeah, Laurie your
dicks so big' *(impression)*

KATHERINE
You know, groans like 'mmm'
(Impression)

LAURIE
'Laurie I can't wait for you to fuck
me, oooh mm'

(Impression *slap face gently with mic
*insinuating a 'dick slap')

KATHERINE
Nothing too much, don't want to sound
like an idiot, do I?

LAURIE
Tried my best to get her warmed up,
stuck my fingers down her pants. Tried
to remember what I read on google

KATHERINE
It was super strange

LAURIE
Mike told me that girls love it when
you play with their, you know
(Flickering motion near groin)

KATHERINE
Finally, he was doing something for me

LAURIE
That little bean is fucking hard to
find (react facing audience) but
didn't take me long to find it. She
loved it

KATHERINE

Not sure if he knew what he was
looking for, I kinda had to guide his
hand. He was actually doing alright at
it at first

LAURIE

I read on google that girls like it
when you flick it *(Impression)*

KATHERINE

Holy shit what was his problem? It was
like he was attempted to flick it off
my actually vagina and across the room

LAURIE

I'm not sure if she liked the flicking
in hindsight, I couldn't tell if she
had angry eyes or horny eyes. Kinda
the same with girls ain't it?

KATHERINE

Fucking idiot. He was out of breath,
he looked down and asked me 'Can I
slip it in now please?'

LAURIE

Then she was like 'Laurie babe, you
gotta fuck me right now. You've made
me so horny'. She was begging for it

KATHERINE

He was actually asking for it

LAURIE
She gave me those sexy eyes, I just
knew I had to rip her tiny top off

KATHERINE
He started pulling at my top like a
mad man, didn't want him to get
embarrassed so I unhooked it at the
back without him noticing

LAURIE
I yanked it off with one pull

KATHERINE
He then tugged at my trousers, I
assumed he wanted me to strip

LAURIE
She then stood up and started slowly
taking her trousers off. She was
practically doing a strip tease

KATHERINE
And all of a sudden, I was naked

LAURIE
She was naked, so I did the same

KATHERINE
His body looked so different to what I
expected

LAURIE
There were a lovely pair of tits

KATHERINE
His balls just kinda, hung there

LAURIE
Her beautiful tits just hung there

KATHERINE
I had no idea what to do next

LAURIE
She just stood there, got the vibe she
wanted me to touch her tits

KATHERINE
He looked at me blankly and then just
kinda placed his hands on my boobs

LAURIE
You know, massaged them, played with
the nipples (impression)

KATHERINE
It felt like a juggling motion, tried
doing something with my nipples like
they were dials on a radio (give
impression) By this point I just
wanted it over with

                    LAURIE
          I never wanted it to end

                   KATHERINE
       I laid down, waiting for him to do it

                    LAURIE
         She asked me if I'd brought a condom

                   KATHERINE
        The idiot didn't even bring a condom.
        Everyone knows it's the lad's job to
                 bring a condom...

                    LAURIE
                    Woops

                   KATHERINE
                 Fucking idiot

                    LAURIE
        We just used the pull out technique

                   KATHERINE
        I remember Rachel saying that the pull
        out technique works like a charm. So
        we gave that a go, no point in
                stopping is there?

                    LAURIE
        I climbed on top her to put it in

KATHERINE
He had no idea what he was doing

LAURIE:
Where is this fucking hole?

KATHERINE
Go up a bit

LAURIE
No that's not right

KATHERINE
Bit to your left

LAURIE
still doesn't feel right

KATHERINE
It's not that difficult!

LAURIE
Oh, wait, I think I found it!

KATHERINE
Woah! It's definitely not there!

LAURIE
Oh shit

KATHERINE
I just grabbed it and shoved it in,
sick of waiting (*LAURIE react*)

LAURIE
Pfft, hole in one

KATHERINE
Okay, we were actually doing it

LAURIE
Oh fuck me, this feels good *(continues
to groan)*

KATHERINE
Oooh I'm not sure how this feels

LAURIE
Yes *(continues to groan louder)*

KATHERINE
Bit faster

LAURIE
Oh god yes *(louder)*

KATHERINE
bit harder

LAURIE
Holy shit!

KATHERINE
A bit… wait

LAURIE
Crap

KATHERINE
he'd finished

LAURIE
That was mint

KATHERINE
that was shit

LAURIE
She defo had an orgasm

KATHERINE
Out of the 3 years we were together he
never made me orgasm

LAURIE
Agree to disagree. It was my first
time, I lasted about thirty minutes

KATHERINE
he lasted about 30 seconds

LAURIE
Best thirty minutes of my life

KATHERINE:
Worst thirty seconds of my life

KATHERINE/ LAURIE
And that's how I lost my virginity

                    LAURIE
        Hands down. Wouldn't change a thing
                   about it

                   KATHERINE
                     Hmm

                    ETHAN
                  Well Kat…

                   KATHERINE
             Don't call me that

                    ETHAN
                 Katherine…
       If you ever need a good experience,
       I'm still in this city for university.
            I can give you my number

        Laurie looks angry at Ethan

                   KATHERINE
                   …What?

                    ETHAN
        Yepp, just a message away if you need
                 a special buddy

                   KATHERINE
               Special buddy?

                    ETHAN
        You know, like a 'helping hand'

KATHERINE
Please stop

LAURIE
I need another drink

Laurie walks past Ethan and stamps on his foot

ETHAN
Ouch! That's my foot man

LAURIE
Oh, was it? I didn't realise…

ETHAN
What about you Jess? What was your first time like?

HOLLY
Rude, you shouldn't just assume someone has done it

ETHAN
I'm just saying, we've heard about everyone's story apart from hers. It's almost like it's a running theme

ETHAN looks at the audience

KATHERINE
I guess he has a point, do you have a
story?

JESS
To the audience
These people seem very confident in
when and how they lost their
virginity. I can't say I'm the same on
the other hand. I guess I'll tell you
my story and then you can decide,
because to this day I'm still unsure
in which instance would class as
'losing my virginity'.

I think what would make it easier for
you all to understand is….

ETHAN
A physical demonstration?

JESS
To just be straight with you, well
not straight. Slightly bent. You see,
I'm bisexual. Nothing exciting, I'm
just attracted to males and females. I
know what you're thinking, is she just
saying that because she's not ready to
come out as a lesbian?

JESS

No, but do I wish I met a woman who
loved to bake. Who has a cottage and a
golden labrador and in the evening we
discuss poetry and books. Absolutely.
But unfortunately it isn't one of
those peeking out the closet before
bursting out sort of situation.

But Jess, how did you know you bend
both ways, I sense you questioning.
From what I can remember, it all
started when I was a young child,
around the age of six. My mother had a
beautiful tradition of making me watch
'Joseph The Technicolor Dreamcoat'
when I felt ill. The bright colours
and music distracted me from feeling
rubbish. Now, this was back when
videos were a thing, we're talking
early 2000's, it was a nostalgic time.
I remember the character Joseph being
imprisoned, with his luscious long
wavy hair and abs that could blind any
female.. Or male, I wouldn't blame
anyone. Obviously I was madly in love
with him, but what surprised me the
most was seeing the female narrator.
Wow, I was entranced by her. It was
confusing. I said to my mum, 'Wow,
she's as beautiful as Joseph!'.

JESS'S MOTHER
Yes, I imagine all the men thinking
she's pretty!

JESS
But why only men? Why couldn't I find
her pretty to the same standard I
found Joseph handsome? My poor mother
probably didn't understand that this
is what I meant, I don't believe a
parent's first thought when their six
year old child says this is… 'And
you're gay'. But at the time, I would
have been happy to marry either of
them.

I spent quite a few years playing a
game in my head when I watched
something on the television, it was
basically 'Would you rather?', and I
would choose if I'd marry the boy or
the girl on the TV. I told my friends
about this game and from their
reaction it seemed that they had never
indulged in such antics.

As I got older, I got more confused.
It probably didn't help that I had
older brothers either.

*Actors set up a dining table within
the scene, mum and two brothers sit
down*

ADAM
So, is dad at work tonight?

JESS'S MOTHER
Yepp, he's on a late one

DERRICK
Is he working with Mandy tonight?

JESS
Who's Mandy?

JESS'S MOTHER
No one, just someone your dad works
with

ADAM
She's a milf that brings extra food
for dad during their lunch break

JESS'S MOTHER
Adam!

DERRICK
She is a bit of a milf though mum

JESS'S MOTHER
Yes, she's a very bonny woman. But
she's married

ADAM
I'd marry her

DERRICK
Same

JESS
Same?

*The room goes quiet, the family looks
at JESS for a moment. They begin to
laugh*

JESS
What?

ADAM
You always do this Jess

JESS
Do what?

ADAM
You just agree with me and Derrick to
fit in. But you can't marry her you
idiot

JESS
Why not?

DERRICK
You're not a lesbian Jess

JESS
What is a lesbian?

The brothers laugh

JESS'S MOTHER
Boys, don't laugh at her. Sweetie, a
lesbian is when one woman loves
another woman..

*As mum is speaking ADAM gestures a
scissoring motion with both his hands*

JESS'S MOTHER
Adam stop, not at the table!

JESS
I could be a lesbian

DERRICK
You can't Jess, lesbians have to eat
lemons and you don't like lemons

JESS
Lemons?

DERRICK
Yes, les-bians…Le-mons? I can't
believe you didn't know that

JESS'S MOTHER
Boys, leave her alone. It's getting
late, start getting ready for bed

The family clear the table and move it from the scene

                    JESS
What was I meant to believe, I was
young compared to them. I went to
catholic school. At this stage I would
have believed anything. I plundered
along my early teens, just secretly
questioning myself every…single…day.

I said to myself, it's just a stage. I
had boyfriends in school, I enjoyed
kissing them so I must want to be with
a boy. I remember a priest once saying
                to us in mass…

                   PRIEST
The devil sends sneaky tricks to us
to attempt to make us sin, therefore
we must always be aware of the dangers
and to remember to listen to God's
                teachings!

                    JESS
Maybe it was the devil itself
attempting to make me sin, I know it
sounds stupid. But this is what
happens when you send your child to
            catholic school.

I ignored every urge and thought when it came to girls. Until I was watching the music channel and heard it. It was like a gay calling…

Intro to Shania Twain 'Man I feel like a woman starts (first six counts) JESS looks around confused. The song restarts again and plays the song. JESS seems awkward at first as the song goes on. She becomes more comfortable as the song goes on, she picks up props and starts to dance to the chorus in an embarrassing manner. Near the end both of the brothers walk in on her and watch in discomfort. After the first chorus ends she notices them and shouts in shock

ADAM
I don't know Derrick, she might be a lesbian. She's looking pretty gay right now

DERRICK
No, I reckon she's attention seeking still

They leave the scene laughing

JESS

Why couldn't I just figure out who or
what I was. Did I want to be Shania
Twain, or did I want to be WITH Shania
Twain? I guess to this day the answer
is both. Always both.

There was only one person in the world
that seemed to understand me, my
friend Maya

MAYA

I agree, I would marry Shania Twain.
Then I could borrow her clothes

JESS
You'd marry a girl?

MAYA
I mean, I guess

*There is a short silence, Jess
whispers*

JESS
Do you like lemons?

JESS turns to the audience

JESS
At this age I knew lesbians didn't
have to eat lemons, but I might as
well ask the question

MAYA
Erm, yes? I like lemon. What a weird
question

JESS
Years went on, Maya and I stayed good
friends

MAYA
I'm just saying, If Jason wanted
wanted to kiss her he should have just
done it at the party

JESS
But how would you even go about that?

MAYA
Easy, you just need to know what you
want

*MAYA reenacts the scene if she was in
the situation, she walks up to JESS
and puts her hair behind her ear, her
hand lingers close to JESS's face*

MAYA
You look beautiful

JESS
I do?

She pulls away from JESS

MAYA
Yes, that's probably what he would
have said to her. Sometimes people
just need a bit of confidence.
Anyways, we should get to bed, it's
getting late

JESS
Sure, I'll just get the bedding from
the cupboard so you're comfortable on
the floor

MAYA
Or I could just sleep in your bed, if
that's ok?

JESS
Yeah, ok

*They both walk off stage, after a
moment mum shouts off stage*

MUM
Maya! Your mum is here to pick you up!

JESS and MAYA walk back onto stage

MAYA
So I'll see you at school tomorrow?

JESS
I guess

MAYA
Are you ok?

JESS
I think I'm just a bit confused, about
what happened last night

MAYA
It was just two friends having fun.
It's not like we had sex or anything,
I told you, girls can't have sex

JESS
Right...

MAYA kisses JESS

MAYA
I'll see you tomorrow

MAYA exits the stage*

JESS

She was right, I did see her tomorrow.
But not as my friend. Not as anything.
She blocked me out, she avoided eye
contact at all costs and spent as much
time away from me as possible. I
didn't know what I did wrong, it
wasn't until I was older I realised
that I actually hadn't done anything
wrong, I think she was just confused.
I mean, I was confused too. But you
know what we do when we're confused?
We go to google!

I searched, and I searched until I
stumbled onto the answer. Bisexual.
Worst part is, there was no changing
me. I tried, I googled, apparently
nothing can change your sexuality.
Apart from conversion therapy…
'allegedly', let's not even delve into
that lie…

Now there was a word for it, now it
was an actual thing. You think I'd
feel better knowing a bit more about
myself, but I didn't. It felt like a
dirty secret.

Jess's comes onto stage

                    JESS'S MOTHER
          Now Sweetie, after school make sure
          you go to your grandads for tea. I'll
                  pick you up for 7pm

                        JESS
                         Ok
          JESS goes to leave

                    JESS'S MOTHER
                        Bye!

          JESS looks shocked

                        JESS
                       What?

                    JESS'S MOTHER
                        Bye?

                        JESS
             No, it's not… I'm not

                    JESS'S MOTHER
             You're not what sweetie?

                        JESS
          Nothing, I thought you said something
                        else

                    JESS'S MOTHER
          Nope, just saying bye. I'll see you
                       later

Mum leaves the scene

JESS
The thing is, bi people don't always
have to confront their internalised
homophobia right away. We can just
hide away, it's socially easier than
being gay. When you're gay you don't
really have a choice, you want to be
with someone who is the same gender.
But bi, I could hide my secret away
for the rest of my life. Marry a man,
have children and then die peacefully.
No one would ever know. Except me.
What a sad existence that sounded
like, hiding who you are from the
people you love.

But that is the life I decided to live
for a while. I met Matt in my late
teens. He was nice, but he was naive.
Our first time was…ok. Nothing like
the horror stories you might hear, in
retrospect it was a bit boring, but no
first time with someone is perfect. We
got close, told each other things
about ourselves that we hadn't told
anyone. I thought this is the perfect
person to tell my secret to. He said
he'd love me no matter what. So I did,
I told him.

                    MATT
             So you like women?

                    JESS
                    Yes

                    MATT
                  And men?

                    JESS
                    Yepp

                    MATT
       So you'd like to do sexy stuff with a
                   woman?

                    JESS
          If that's how you want to put it

                    MATT
        So are you like, into threesomes?

                    JESS
                Really Matt?

                    MATT
       I'm just asking because bisexual
     people have the reputation of having
     threesomes. I mean I wouldn't say no
       if that is something you are into

                    JESS
    Matt, I just want to be with you
                 right now

                    MATT
    And you're definitely not a lesbian

                    JESS
                    No

    *MATT nods as if he is still working
       out what was said to him*

                    JESS
    It was working fine, I did feel over
    sexualised though when he told his
    friends. They asked horrid questions
    and he just sat there, smirking. It
    made me feel uncomfortable, I wasn't
    some hypersexualised being that fucked
    everything that had a pulse.

    As time went on, Matt started to
    become concerned of my sexuality

                    MATT
    So I was already worried you'd cheat
    on me with a dude. But now you can
    cheat on me with a woman. It's like
    double the chance of you cheating on
                    me

JESS
I'm not going to cheat on you,
regardless of my sexuality. Why would
you think that?

The irony is, it wasn't me who cheated
in this relationship. It was him

MATT leaves the scene

JESS
So, I did what any sane person would
do after a situation like this. I
invited my friends over to have a
bitch and moan about him.

CHLOE
He is such an asshole

AMY
Yes, such an asshole

JESS
I just want to forget he existed, he
was so shit in bed

CHLOE
That doesn't surprise me. Men at this
age don't care if we enjoy sex

                    AMY
They literally just want to get their
              dick wet

                    JESS
So gross, but true. I should just be
              with a woman

                    AMY
A woman? At least they'd actually pay
attention to you during sex. Just out
         of interest, is Adam in?

                    JESS
Yeah? He's in his room. Why?

                    AMY
No reason, I'm just off to the toilet.
          I'll be back soon

Amy exits

                   CHLOE
You know she's off to go find your
              brother?

                    JESS
Yeah, I know…

CHLOE
Anyways, I wonder what it's like being
with a girl. I mean I kissed one or
two when I've been drunk but I don't
think I could have sex with one. Have
you ever been with a woman Jess?

JESS
I mean, kind of

CHLOE
No way! You have to tell me the
details

JESS
I can't

CHLOE
Yes you can! Come on, don't be shy. I
won't tell anyone. Just whisper what
happened in my ear if that makes you
feel better

*JESS whispers in her ear, Chloe looks
shocked*

CHLOE
Jess, I didn't know you had sex with
a girl!

                    JESS
What? Sex? No, girls can't have sex
          with each other

                   CHLOE
What world do you live in? Of course
they can, and what you just told me is
                    sex

Amy re-enters

                    AMY
          What did I miss?

                   CHLOE
Jess has had sex with a girl!

                    AMY
               What!?

                    JESS
               Chloe!

                    AMY
Wait, so did this happen before or
after Matt? Like did you hop straight
            to another bed?

                    JESS
No, it happened before Matt

                    AMY
    So you lost your virginity to a girl?

                    JESS
                  No, wait

                   CHLOE
    Look, I've been on redtube and what
you described is what happens when you
    type in girls having sex with other
                    girls

                    JESS
    But I lost my virginity to Matt…

                   CHLOE
    Hm, I don't think you did… Come on,
    let's get some more food from
downstairs and I'll show you it on
                  redtube…

The friends exit

JESS

Was I wrong about my first time? for
so many years? I mean, I don't regret
being with Maya, or with Matt. But I
had my 'first time' story, I had told
that story so many times. Now it's
different. Is it different? I didn't
even know that was sex. Maya said
girls can't have sex with other girls.
God I was naive. But my friends didn't
judge me, sure they were surprised.
But they didn't look disgusted at me.
I thought 'fuck it'. I told my family,
and to my surprise I had the most
boring but also lovely responses.

DERRICK

I fucking knew you was gay, Adam owes
me a tenner

ADAM

Actually she's half gay, which means I
only owe you £5

JESS'S MOTHER

As long as they treat you well that's
all that matters. I think if your
father ever passes away I might date a
woman to see what it's like.

                    JESS
To this day, I don't fully know how to
   answer that question. Was my first
 time with Maya or Matt? Actually, does
  it really matter? What difference to
 my life does it make with what answer
   I give. Surely it really makes no
  difference to me, or anyone for that
                   matter.

   All I know is that I enjoyed both
  experiences. So, that's my story. No
  definitive answer. So I guess you can
 decide what the answer is, not like I
  give a shit. I'm just happy I'm at a
 stage in life where I am what I am. A
               bisexual woman.

                   ETHAN
                   Nice

                  LAURIE
          Don't be gross Ethan

                  HOLLY
Gosh is that what time it is? I should
               be going

                   JESS
   You're right, I can see the sun
 starting to rise through the window

KATHERINE
That's the streetlight outside

JESS
Oh, maybe I should call this my last
drink

KATHERINE
You're right, we're into the early
hours of the morning

HOLLY
Come on Jess, you can share a taxi
with me

ETHAN
What? I've come to the last party of
the academic year and I'm not going to
spend the night with a girl?

LAURIE
The only woman you're spending the
night with is your mother. Now come
on, it's time to go home

JESS
Thanks for having me Katherine

KATHERINE
Thanks for coming, you're actually
really great to hang with

ETHAN
I guess I'll see you around

Ethan goes to hug Katherine goodbye

KATHERINE
Absolutely not

HOLLY
Well, I guess I'll probably see you at
Christmas for the family boxing day
party

KATHERINE
You'll see me sooner, I'm going to
make sure I come to visit you. I know
you're going to struggle not having me
around

HOLLY
Yeah, sure

They all leave, apart from Laurie

KATHERINE
I bet you're excited to get going

LAURIE
From the party?

KATHERINE
From this city idiot

LAURIE
There's going to be a few things I
miss

KATHERINE
Like?

LAURIE
People

KATHERINE
Who?

Laurie looks at Katherine

LAURIE
You know what I've always admired
about you Katherine?

You have some sort of sparkle in your
eyes, I did love seeing that everyday

KATHERINE
It dulled a bit, but I think I'll get
it back soon

*Laurie goes to leave but then turns
back*

                    LAURIE
I know that we're a mess, but hear me
out. We knew when it was going to be
our first time together. But we never
knew when it was going to be our last.
What if we made our last time count
              for something

                   KATHERINE
        You want to stay the night?

                    LAURIE
      Do you want me to stay the night?

They get closer

                   KATHERINE
      If you stay the night, you'll only
          leave again in the morning

                    LAURIE
    But we'd separate on a good memory

*They go into a kiss but before it
happens Katherine stops.*

                   KATHERINE
You were right though Laurie. We were
  made to break, and I'm ok with that

                    LAURIE
                    Right

                    KATHERINE
I'm happy you came to the party, but
I'm going to bed alone tonight. It's
          the right thing to do

                     LAURIE
                      Ok

                   KATHERINE
             Get home safe Laurie

                     LAURIE
            Sweet dreams Katherine